5 Steps to
Win Her Heart

PRAISE FOR *STORYSHARES*

"One of the brightest innovators and game-changers in the education industry."
– Forbes

"Your success in applying research-validated practices to promote literacy serves as a valuable model for other organizations seeking to create evidence-based literacy programs."
- Library of Congress

"We need powerful social and educational innovation, and Storyshares is breaking new ground. The organization addresses critical problems facing our students and teachers. I am excited about the strategies it brings to the collective work of making sure every student has an equal chance in life."
– Teach For America

"Around the world, this is one of the up-and-coming trailblazers changing the landscape of literacy and education."
- International Literacy Association

"It's the perfect idea. There's really nothing like this. I mean wow, this will be a wonderful experience for young people."   - Andrea Davis Pinkney, Executive Director, Scholastic

"Reading for meaning opens opportunities for a lifetime of learning. Providing emerging readers with engaging texts that are designed to offer both challenges and support for each individual will improve their lives for years to come. Storyshares is a wonderful start."
- David Rose, Co-founder of CAST & UDL

5 Steps to Win Her Heart

Natasha Lopez

Story Share, Inc.
New York. Boston. Philadelphia.

Storyshares
Story Share, Inc.
24 N. Bryn Mawr Avenue #340
Bryn Mawr, PA 19010-3304
www.storyshares.org

Inspiring reading with a new kind of book.

Interest Level: High School
Grade Level Equivalent: 1.3

9798885979252

Book design by Storyshares

Printed in the United States of America

Storyshares Presents

1

It's the year 2002, and middle school is **weird.**

I used to be Luke Skywalker. Then, I turned hairy. My arms grew down to my kneecaps. My voice got low and scratchy. Now, I'm
Chewbacca . . . well, **almost.** I'm still short, and I still have a baby tooth. Kat changed too.

Kat Nguyen was my best friend and girlfriend. Kat loved Star Wars and football. She never cried when she got tackled. Not one tear! Then, she grew tall and pretty. I stayed short and ugly. Now, she's kissing Josh Fowler in front of the sci-fi books.

Do they have to kiss in front of the only books that aren't boring?

"Excuse me," I say.

Kat and Josh don't move. As I reach for my book, my knee hits the back of Kat's head.

"Ouch!" Kat stops and rubs her head. Josh's eyes are still closed. His lips are shiny with spit.

"What book are you looking for, Mateo?" Kat asks.

I point to the top shelf.

Josh laughs like a villain. "What's wrong, Yoda? Are you too short to reach?"

"Judge me by my size, do you?" I say quietly. "The stupid is strong with this one."

Kat laughs so hard she snorts and chokes on her breath.

"You sound like a donkey," Josh complains.

Kat covers her mouth. Kat never had to hide her laugh when she was dating me.

She hands me *Star Wars: Episode I – The Phantom Menace.*

"Did you see the new movie, *Attack of the Clones*?" she asks.

"I did," I reply. "The romance was a little weird."

"No way! It was *so* sweet!" She tucks her shiny black hair behind her ear. "Plus, Anakin is *so* hot."

"I'm still here," Josh complains.

I ignore him. "You think *Darth Vader* is hot?"

Kat rolls her eyes. "He's not Darth Vader yet. He's *Anakin.*"

Mrs. Reed appears behind Josh and Kat. She snaps her fingers.

"You only have ten minutes to check out a book. Go! Go! Go!"

You know Jabba the Hutt from *Return of the Jedi*? He's the one that looks like a giant booger. Mrs. Reed doesn't look like a booger, but she does kinda look like Jabba the Hutt.

Mrs. Reed frowns at my book. "Star Wars *again,* Mateo? Why don't you pick something more educational?"

Because then I would never read! I almost say, but I don't.

Mrs. Reed walks away. Josh kisses Kat's ear and whispers, "Ten minutes is enough time for another kiss."

Kat holds her ear and laughs like a little girl. I've never heard her sound like that. Middle school really is **weird.**

2

I take my book to the librarian to check out. The librarian's name is Mr. Y. He told us to call him Mr. Y because his last name is hard to say. I think the "Y" stands for Mr. Yoda because he is probably the oldest man I've ever seen.

Mr. Y points to the stack of books beside him. "Wait a minute. I have to get these books checked in."

There's like a hundred books in that pile!

Mr. Y takes a book from the top of the stack. He flips through the pages with shaky hands. Slowly, he unfolds each dog-eared page.

This is going to take forever! I only have one book. Just check out my book! I almost say aloud.

My best friend Diego gets in line behind me. He looks over my shoulder. "You like *Star Wars*?"

"Yeah . . . what's wrong with that?" I ask.

He shrugs. "It was weird how Luke Skywalker fell in love with his sister."

My voice is loud. "Luke did NOT fall in love with his sister! Did you even watch the movies?!"

Diego holds his hands up. "Calm down! I only watched the first one!"

I take a deep breath.

Diego grins. "I like this side of you, Mateo. You're usually a doormat."

"A *doormat*?"

Diego nods. "You let people step on you. Like when you let Josh steal Kat."

"I didn't *let* Josh steal Kat. She dumped me." My voice isn't loud anymore. I don't like the way it sounds.

"You should try to win her back." Diego stops and thinks. "Be like Han Solo. He's cool, right?"

"Kat doesn't like Han. She thinks he's a jerk."

"Really?" Diego scratches his head. "Then, why is she

dating Josh?"

"I don't know." I throw my arms out.

Finally, Mr. Y reaches for my book. "Thank you for waiting," he says.

"Maybe you can be like another Star Wars character, then?" Diego continues.

"What's wrong with being me?" I ask.

"I don't know," he shrugs. "Ask Kat. She's the one who dumped you."

Ouch.

Mrs. Reed claps her hands together. "Times up! Line up class!"

Diego rushes to the front of the line. I follow him. Mr. Y calls out to me, "Don't forget your book!"

"Oops! Sorry!" I return to take the *Star Wars* book from his wrinkly hand.

There's a small book tucked under my *Star Wars book*. It's titled, *5 Steps to Win Her Heart!* The pages are brown and yellow and ripped. There's stick figures of a boy and girl on the cover. A big red heart glows between them.

I give Mr. Y the book. He pushes it away.

"I didn't check out this book," I say.

"I know," Mr. Y replies.

I stare at him. "So, can I give it back?"

"Do you want to give it back?"

"Um . . . yes?"

He stares at me. "Are you sure?"

Is this a trick question? I almost ask.

"I think you could learn something from that book."

I sigh and put the book under my arm. "I guess I'll give it a try . . ." "Do or don't do. There is no try," Mr. Y says in a Yoda voice.

Mr. Y knows *Star Wars*! I'm so surprised I almost don't hear Mrs. Reed calling me.

"Mateo! Let's go!" she yells.

On the way to class, I skim through Mr. Y's book. I smile to myself.

Middle school is **weird**, but maybe that's a good thing.

3

The school bus drops me off a few blocks from my house. Mom wishes the bus would drop me off closer. I don't. I like walking with Trey.

Treyvone Evans is my other best friend. He's taller than most of the seventh graders. He's good at sports. He could be one of the cool kids, but he talks about *Star Wars* too much.

A few days ago, I was sleeping over at Trey's house. Trey made an X-Wing Fighter out of cardboard. He tied the cardboard to his back and said he would fly.

"The Force is with me!" he'd said.

I remember shaking my head. "I don't think that's a good idea."

In a Darth Vader voice, he'd replied, "I find your lack of faith disturbing." Then, he'd jumped off the roof.

The Force had not been with Trey.

"Pew! Pew! Pew!" I hear laser sounds. An acorn flies into my face, just missing my eyeball.

"Ouch! Ouch! Stop!" I yell as more and more acorns strike me.

"Then, stop daydreaming and get up here!" Trey waves at me from inside the Galactic Oak.

The Galactic Oak is an old deer hunting fort. Trey, Kat, and I found it in the fourth grade. We fixed the holes in the floor where long tree branches broke through. We painted a plastic tarp to look like R2D2. Then, we nailed the tarp to the roof so rain wouldn't get in.

The tarp was Kat's idea.

I climb into the Galactic Oak. "I thought you were still in the hospital?"

"The doctor let me leave early," Trey replies.

"How's your leg?"

Trey puts his foot in my face. "Look! I got a cool cast! It's neon blue like Luke's lightsaber."

I scoot away from his foot. "How did you get up here?"

"I used the Force!" he says proudly.

I stare at him. "Did your sister help you?"

"I *told* you! I used the Force!" Trey points to my backpack. "Is my homework in there?"

I pull out Trey's math book and homework packets. Mr. Y's book slides in front of Trey.

"What's this?" he asks.

"Nothing!" I say quickly.

"Wow! This book was written in 1955!" Trey flips through the pages. "This is hilarious. Listen to this."

I reach for the book. Trey holds it over his head.

"Give it back! I need that!"

"Why? Are you trying to win Kat's heart?" He says it like he's joking.

My face gets hot. My ears feel like they're on fire. "So what if I am?!"

Trey freezes. I grab the book, throw it in my backpack, and zip it up.

"Are you serious?" he asks.

I hug my backpack close to my chest. "Maybe . . ."

Trey opens his mouth to say something. He stops himself. "You don't think I can, do you?" I ask. "You think I'm a doormat."

"Nooo . . ." Trey makes the "O" sound for too long.

"I'm going home." I go down the first step of the ladder.

"Wait," Trey pulls me back up by my backpack.

I punch Trey in the arm. "Let me go!"

We battle in the Galactic Oak. I pin Trey by the arms, but he pushes me off easily. Then, he pulls me by my leg like the Wampa pulls Luke through the snow.

I can't lose to a guy with a broken leg!

I grab Trey's math book and throw it at his cast. Trey moves just in time.

"Are you crazy?!" he yells.

"You wouldn't let me leave!" I yell back.

"I stopped you because I think you *should* win Kat back," he says.

I stare at him. "Are you lying?"

"Of course not!" He shakes his head. "I think you're way better for Kat than *Darth Josh.*"

"*Darth* Josh?"

"Josh is definitely part of the Dark Side."

I nod.

Trey points to my backpack. "Show me the first step in that book."

I take out the book and flip to the first page. I read the first step out loud: "Step 1. Take good care of your body. Comb your hair and keep your clothes neat and clean. No girl likes a wrinkly Todd!"

"What's a *Todd?*" Trey asks.

"I think it's another word for boy," I reply.

Trey looks at me. His eyes go up and down. "I think you already do this part."

"Okay, let's go to the next step." I turn the page.

Trey turns it back. "Kat dumped you even though you do the first step," he says.

I roll my eyes. "I *know* that. Let's move on." I turn the page.

Trey turns it back again. "You need to do *more*." He points to my shirt. "Change your look. Dress like someone Kat likes."

I remember what Kat said in the library. "She likes Anakin."

Trey snaps his fingers. "That's it! Make yourself look like

Anakin!"

"How?" I ask. "I don't look anything like him."

Trey taps his chin. "Your dad has a cool leather belt you could borrow."

"I . . . don't think that's enough."

Trey looks at the white stars painted on the ceiling and thinks and thinks for a long time. Then, he smiles. I don't like the way he smiles.

Trey points to my hair.

I shake my head. "No."

Trey wiggles his finger. "You want to date Kat again, don't you?"

I shake my head some more. "My mom will kill me!"

"Get your butt down here, Treyvone William Evans!" Mrs. Evans calls out.

Trey shrinks down like he just saw Darth Vader. "I better go!" He grabs his books and homework packets. Before he hobbles down the stairs, he points to his hair.

"No," I repeat.

He smiles. "Think about it."

"Be careful with that foot!" Mrs. Evans holds her arms out in case Trey falls. He finds the ground safely.

"How did you even get up there?" Mrs. Evans asks. "Was it Raquelle? Did your sister help you?"

"Yes . . ." Trey says quietly, but I still hear him.

I knew it. I knew his sister helped him.

Mrs. Evans sees me in the Galactic Oak. She calls out, "Mateo, hurry home before it gets dark!"

"Yes, Mrs. Evans," I reply.

The red sun and the white streetlight shine on my bedroom window. The sky is pink and purple like on planet Tatooine before Luke's life changed forever.

I think about what Trey said. I think about what Mr. Y said. I think about what Diego said. I think about Kat.

Maybe I **should** change my look.

4

Why did I listen to a guy who thought he could fly?

I pull my hoodie down to my eyebrows as I walk through the crowded seventh-grade hallway.

"Get your books and get out of here as fast as you can," I whisper to myself.

I turn the knob to my locker like a button on a battleship. The lock turns so fast I can't see the numbers.

"Hey, Mateo!" Trey says.

I jump. "Don't sneak up on me like that!"

"You need to slow down." Trey opens my locker for me. I hurry and grab my homework and books.

"The hoodie looks cool," he says, "but you look more like

a Jawa than Anakin."

"You weren't on the bus," I say quietly.

"What?" Trey puts a hand behind his ear.

"You weren't on the bus," I repeat a little louder. "I *needed* you."

Trey looks confused. "Why?"

I pull Trey behind the vending machine.

"What's going on? You're acting weird," he says.

"*Me?* Acting weird?" I laugh.

"A little bit," he laughs nervously.

"Josh attacked me on the bus!" I say.

Trey's eyes get big, "He hit you?"

I look around. Then, I whisper, "Josh tried to pull my hoodie off!"

"That's it?" Trey sighs. "Just put your hoodie back on. What's the big deal?"

"The big deal is *this!*" I pull my hoodie off. Trey jumps backward.

"What happened?!" he asks.

"*You* did this!" I complain.

"I told you to look like Anakin." He points to my head. "Not that!"

I pull the hoodie back on. "Help me get to class without Kat seeing me!"

Trey looks around the corner. He looks right, left, up, and down. Then, he whispers, "All clear!"

I step out and bump into Josh's chest.

"Watch where you're going, Yoda!" he says.

I shoot Trey an angry look.

Trey throws his hands out. "You said to look for Kat, not Josh!"

"Did someone say my name?" Kat steps out from behind Josh.

No. No. **No!**

I walk away as fast as I can.

"Wait! You dropped this!" Kat holds out my homework packet. A homework sheet falls out. Kat and I bonk heads as we reach for it.

"Ouch!" we both say.

I look up. Kat's face is an inch from mine. Her eyes are so beautiful...

"Stop staring at my girlfriend!" Josh pulls me back by my hoodie. I slip on the homework sheet.

"Mateo!" Kat and Trey yell at the same time.

As I fall, I remember how I ended up in this mess.

I remember Dad brushing my hair with his fingers. I remember bleached white hair falling right off my head. I remember mom's voice, "*Ay, Dios mio!* Mateo! What have you done?!"

I fall flat on my back. Kat picks me up. She holds me like Luke holds Darth Vader in *Return of the Jedi*. In that scene, Luke takes Darth Vader's mask off. Kat doesn't take my hoodie off. It slides off by itself.

The hallway gets quiet. The only thing I can hear is my loud breathing. Ashley O'Connell points at me with one long, red fingernail.

"He's bald!" she yells.

Everyone starts laughing.

If Darth Vader was in 7th grade, I think he would have kept his mask on.

Josh gets too close to my face. His breath burns my nose hairs as he asks, "Do I get three wishes if I rub your head?"

Josh rubs my head with his elbow. Kat yanks his arm

backward.

"Hey!" Josh complains.

"Leave him alone!" she says. I've never seen her look so angry.

Josh puts his arm around her shoulders. "Come on, Kat! He looks like an idiot!"

Kat pushes his arm off. She looks at me. Then she looks at Josh. "He looks a million times cooler than *you*." She storms away. Josh hurries to catch her.

Trey shakes his head. "I can't believe it."

"Me neither," I reply.

Kat said I'm cool. Kat said **I'm cool!**

"Step 1 worked!" Trey pats me on the back. "What's the next step?"

I take out Mr. Y's book. Trey grabs it and reads the second step out loud:

"Step 2. Join a sport. A girl wants to know she is safe and protected. Sports are a great way to show off your physical strength!"

Trey flips through the rest of the book. Then he looks around.

"What are you doing?" I ask.

He rips a sheet off the bulletin board.

"Uh, I don't think you're allowed to do that." I reach for the paper. Trey holds the sheet up to my nose.

"Football tryouts are today after school!" Trey says excitedly.

"I don't know about this." I push Trey's hand away. "I like football, but I'm not good at it."

"You have the Force on your side!" He grins. "After tryouts, you can ask Kat to the dance this weekend."

My hands get sweaty. "Isn't that too soon?" Trey hands me Mr. Y's book. "Read step 3."

I read the third step out loud:

"Step 3. Ask her on a date. The local soda shop is a wonderful spot for a first date. Girls love dinner and dancing!"

"The school dance has dinner *and* dancing," Trey explains.

"Kat's going with Josh," I complain.

Trey shakes the football tryout sheet. "She'll change her mind when you beat Josh at tryouts."

I rub my hands on my pants. "Are you sure?"

Trey puts his hands on my shoulders. "May the Force be with you!"

I look at the cast on Trey's leg. I hope the Force is with **me** more than it was with Trey.

5

I wait on the benches with Josh, Diego, and the other guys trying out. I check the bleachers to see if Kat is still watching. The sun is so bright it hurts to look that way. I've failed at everything so far. I have only one chance left.

Coach yells out, "Josh Fowler versus Mateo Jones! Line up and wait for the whistle!"

The football field smells like wet grass and mud. Josh and I face each other. He's wearing a red jersey while I'm wearing a blue one. We look like Obi-Wan and Darth Vader before their battle in *A New Hope.*

Josh bends low. "Good luck, *baby.*"

"I'm *not* a baby." My voice sounds exactly like a baby

when I say that. *Where's my Chewbacca voice when I need it?*

"You think you're a man?" Josh laughs.

No. Not really, I almost say.

Josh grins. "I'm going to knock all your baby teeth out!"

Coach blows the whistle and throws the football in the air.

My fingers touch the skin of the ball. *I got it!* Josh reaches over my head and grabs the ball. *I don't got it.*

I leap at Josh, but he spins out of the way. I eat mud and grass and rocks as I roll on the ground. The guys on the bench start laughing. I wonder if Kat laughs too.

Josh stands over me. "*Give up!* The odds of beating me are

zero!"

I think he's talking about more than just football.

Don't tell me the odds, I think.

Suddenly, I'm **tired** of not saying things aloud.

I stand up slowly and spit out grass and blood. "Don't tell me the odds!" I yell, loud enough for Josh, Coach, the bench guys, and Kat to hear.

"Run!" the bench guys yell.

Josh runs.

I slide on the wet grass. I swing at the back of Josh's legs like I'm holding a lightsaber. Josh falls flat on his back. The bench guys cheer as I steal the ball and cross the endzone.

Coach blows the whistle. "Excellent job, Mateo!"

I beat Josh at football. *I defeated Josh! Is this how Luke and Han felt when Princess Leia gave them medals? Is Kat excited too?* Now that the sun is behind a cloud, I check the bleachers.

Kat wipes her eyes and hugs her legs. She doesn't look excited at all.

I take off my helmet and go sit down beside her. "Sorry about Josh," I say.

Kat looks up. Her eyes are watery, but they are still the most beautiful eyes I have ever seen.

"Oh... Did something happen to Josh?" she asks.

"Oh, uh, no...." I lie.

Kat looks around. "Where's Trey?"

"His mom got mad at him for going to the Galactic Oak," I reply. "She's picking him up from school every day until his cast is off."

"Oh..." Kat hides her face in her knees.

"You're not sad about the game, are you?" I ask.

"My cat died," she says quietly.

"Mr. Whiskers died?" I try to find the right words. I can't. "I'm really sorry, Kat."

Josh runs over and glares up at me. "What's going on?"

"Her cat died," I reply.

"I wasn't talking to you, Yoda." He touches Kat's shoulder. She moves away. Josh looks annoyed. "What's your problem?" he asks her.

"Mateo already told you! My cat died!"

Josh shrugs. "Sorry, but wasn't he super old? Old cats die."

Kat looks at Josh like Leia looked at Jabba. "You're horrible!"

"I'm still here!" He points to himself. "I'm your boyfriend. You're not paying attention to me at all!"

Josh leans in for a kiss. Again, Kat moves away. "I am *not* your girlfriend! Not anymore!"

"The dance is *this* weekend! There's no way you'll find another date!" Josh yells.

I think about step 3. I hear Mr. Y in my head. He says, *Do or don't do. There is no try!*

I take a deep breath and say, "Kat's going with me!"

Kat looks surprised. "Mateo...you and I broke up."

"We'll go as friends!" I say quickly. That is **not** what I wanted to say!

Josh laughs. "She's not going with you."

"Yes, I am." Kat glares at Josh as she talks to me. "Mateo, I'll go to the dance with you."

Josh's face turns redder than Darth Maul's. Trey was right. The Force **is** with me!

6

Trey sits on the green sofa while mom takes a million pictures of Kat and me.

"How many more pictures, Mom?" I ask. "My face hurts."

"If you smiled more, then your face wouldn't hurt," Mom replies.   Trey leans over and whispers, "She's right. Remember Step 4?"   I whisper the fourth step:

"Step 4. Smile often. A smile makes a face more handsome. You're sure to win her heart with a charming smile!"

I put on the biggest smile.

"Beautiful, *mijo!*" Mom snaps more pictures."Now, look

into each other's eyes!"

Kat looks surprised, then she snorts.

"Your face!" she laughs. "You look so weird!"

I look at myself in the mirror behind us. My cheeks are puffed out. My smile is wider than my face. If Chewbacca ever smiled, this is how he'd look.

"You don't have to smile weird," Kat says. "I like your *real* smile."

My heart leaps in my chest. I feel like I can jump off the roof and fly. I don't even need the Force!

Trey gives me a thumbs up and whispers, "One more step to

go!"

"Smile, Mateo!" Mom says.

"Let them go already." Dad covers the camera lens with his hand. "The dance will be over before they get there."

Mom pulls his fingers off the lens. "Just one more! Look into each other's eyes. Smile!"

"I think my smile is stuck, " Kat says to me.

I laugh.

"*Perfecto!*" Mom puts a hand over her heart. "You look so cute!"   "Mom!" I complain.

"Let me fix your tie." She tightens my red tie like she wants to choke me. "Oh! I should take another picture!"

"No more!" Dad pushes Trey, Kat, and me out the door. "Enjoy your dance!"

The moon in the sky is so bright we don't even need streetlights. The wind blowing through the trees sounds like rain.

"It's cold." Kat hugs herself. "I wish I was wearing pants."   Kat looks just like Padme in her blue dress with her hair curled.

"You look beautiful," I say.

"Thanks," she smiles. "But I still wish I was wearing pants."

Trey pokes me with his elbow and whispers, "Give her your suit jacket."

"Would you like my jacket?" I ask Kat.

"Aren't you cold?" she asks.

"I'm not cold at all," I lie.

"You're a nice guy, Mateo." Kat puts my jacket over her shoulders. My ears feel hot. I'm not cold anymore.

"Wow! They finally picked a cool theme for the dance!"

Trey says as we step inside the gym.

The theme for the dance is "Starry Nights." The ceiling has a million silver stars hanging down on strings. On one side of the gym are tables covered with confetti. On the other side of the gym is the dance floor. A projector makes shiny stars fill the floor. It looks like they're dancing in outer space.

"Hey! It's our hero, Mateo!" The bench guys come over.

"I think your bald head gave you superpowers!" Diego rubs my head. "See you at practice Monday!"

Trey looks surprised. "I didn't know you made the football team!"

"Sorry, I guess I forgot to tell you," I reply.

I forgot because all I could think about after tryouts was Kat.

Kat pulls me by my sleeve. "Let's dance!"

Josh is already on the dance floor when Kat and I get there. He dances with Ashley like a broken C-3PO. He glares at me, but I don't care. I'm the hero.

I'm the one on the football team. I'm the one dancing with the prettiest girl in 7th grade. Tonight, the Force is with **me**!

Kat's eyes sparkle as she says, "I'm glad I came to the dance with you."

"Me too," I reply.

"I'm glad I can be myself!" Kat talks and talks, but all I can think about is the last step:

Step 5. Ask her on another date. Be honest about your feelings. Show her your romantic side!

"Do you want to go on another date?" I ask.   Kat stops talking. She stares at me. "What?"
Maybe she didn't hear me.

"Do you want to go on another date?" I ask louder. A few people look over at us.

Kat stops dancing. "You said we were going to the dance as *friends.*"

"Yeah, but you said you were glad you came to the dance with me," I reply.

"I'm glad I came with you as *friends.*" She plays nervously with her blue dress. "We broke up already, remember?"

No. No. **No!** All the other steps worked! *What am I doing wrong? What did the last part of Step 5 say? I know! I need to show her my romantic side!*

I lean in close to Kat.

"Mateo?! What are you doing?!" She steps back until she's sitting on the bleachers. I get closer and closer.

32

"Stop!" Kat yells.

I kiss her right on the lips the way Han kisses Leia in *The Empire Strikes Back.* Kat doesn't kiss me back. Kat looks angrier than when Josh made fun of me.

She grabs my red tie and throws me down on the bleachers. Then she punches me in the face. I taste blood.

"Oh my gosh!" Ashley points at something on the ground.

Right there in the middle of the dance floor is my very last baby tooth.

Needless to say, the Force is **not** with me.

7

The year is 2003, and middle school is still **weird**. I wish winter break were longer than two weeks. Then maybe everyone would forget about the dance. I wish I could forget.

"I'm returning your book." I give Mr. Y *5 STEPS TO WIN HER HEART!*

'How did it go?" he asks.

Josh walks past me. He sticks his tongue out and pretends to punch himself in the face. His friends do the same thing.

"I think that answers your question," I reply.

"What happened?" Mr. Y asks.

I sigh. "Kat didn't fall in love with me."

Mr. Y stares at me. "Was she supposed to?"

"Isn't that why you gave me the book?" I ask.

Mr. Y shakes his head. "I gave you that book so you would *do* new things instead of *letting* things happen to you. Did it work?"

I think about this. "I dyed my hair." I pause. "Then I lost my hair."

"It looks good on you." Mr. Y says.

I shrug. "You're probably the only one who thinks so."

"Did you do anything else?" he asks.

I think some more. "I joined the football team."

"Did you have fun?"

"I did," I reply.

All the wrinkles on Mr. Y's cheeks lift when he smiles. "Then you have succeeded. May the Force be with you, my young Padawan."

* * *

I climb into the Galactic Oak. I miss Trey. He's probably the only 7th Grader who doesn't think I'm a loser. I miss Kat too. She'll probably never talk to me again.

The air is colder than planet Hoth, but my jacket is warm and cozy. I lay down and fall asleep. When I wake up, Kat is sitting criss-cross in front of me.

"*Why* did you *kiss* me?" she asks.

Am I dreaming?

"Um...what?" I ask.

"*Why* did you kiss me?" Her voice is scary this time.

"I wanted to be romantic," I say quietly.

She glares at me. "I told you no!"

I say even more quietly, "I thought you were pretending. Like Leia."

She rolls her eyes, "You thought you could be like Han and *force* a kiss? Mateo, you know I don't like Han!"

"I know! I know! I was stupid!" I look at Kat in the eyes. "I'm really sorry."

She pulls her knees to her chest. "I don't know if I can forgive you yet."

I nod my head.

We sit together quietly. The birds sing their evening songs.

"Are you dating Josh again?" I ask.

"No. He's a jerk." She looks at me. "You were a jerk too."

"I know," I reply.

Kat looks at the stars painted on the ceiling. "We had a lot of fun here. Didn't we?"

"We did," I reply.

"I want to be friends again." Kat looks at me. "Can we be friends again?"

I look at the pink and purple sky. I look at the white streetlight and the red sun going down over the hill. I look at Kat.

"I think I like you too much to be friends again," I say.

Kat smiles. It's a sad smile. "We can't be kids anymore, can we?"

I quote Anakin's mom, "You can't stop the change, any more than you can stop the suns from setting."

Kat sighs, then stretches. "I should go home before it gets dark."

I watch Kat climb down the steps. Suddenly, there's a weird jumpiness in my legs. I hurry down the ladder so fast I skip the last few steps.

A strong wind rips dead winter leaves off their

branches. They spin in circles around Kat.

"Kat!" I yell.

"Are you okay?" Kat tucks her hair behind her ear.

I hold my hand out in front of me. My fingers spread out wide.   "May the Force be with you," I say.

Kat holds her hand out the same way. She has a big smile on her face.

"May the force be with us all," she replies.

Middle school is weird but, maybe that's a **good** thing.

About The Author

Growing up, Natasha had a chronic case of procrastination. Over time, her symptoms lessened and she was able to complete her first book, "5 Steps to Win Her Heart." She looks forward to creating more thoughtful, humorous, and heartwarming stories for reluctant readers and bookworms alike.

About The Publisher

Story Shares is a nonprofit focused on supporting the millions of teens and adults who struggle with reading by creating a new shelf in the library specifically for them. The ever-growing collection features content that is compelling and culturally relevant for teens and adults, yet still readable at a range of lower reading levels.

Story Shares generates content by engaging deeply with writers, bringing together a community to create this new kind of book. With more intriguing and approachable stories to choose from, the teens and adults who have fallen behind are improving their skills and beginning to discover the joy of reading. For more information, visit storyshares.org.

Easy to Read. Hard to Put Down.

www.ingramcontent.com/pod-product-compliance
Lightning Source LLC
Chambersburg PA
CBHW071226170626
46809CB00005BA/1959